# BILL

*and his*

# *VOYAGE TO WORLD'S END*

The author's grateful thanks to the late Stanley Harris
for composing the music for Beggar Rat's
two songs

# BILL BADGER
## *and the*
# *VOYAGE TO*
# *WORLD'S END*

# 'BB'

MAMMOTH

*Also available from Mammoth*

Bill Badger and the Pirates
The Little Grey Men
The Little Grey Men Go Down the Bright Stream

First published in volume form 1969
by Kaye & Ward Ltd
Published 1993 by Mammoth
an imprint of Reed Consumer Books Ltd
Michelin House, 81 Fulham Road, London SW3 6RB
and Auckland, Melbourne, Singapore and Toronto

Copyright © 1969 'BB'

ISBN 0 7497 1281 3

A CIP catalogue record for this title
is available from the British Library

Printed in Great Britain
by Cox & Wyman Ltd, Reading, Berkshire

# CHAPTER ONE

Matty McVole, the boat builder and hirer of pleasure craft, was busy working in his office. He had been ill and absent from business for some weeks and a lot of letters had to be dealt with. Yet, it was no morning to be stuffing indoors. There was more than a hint of spring in the air.

He sighed and pushed up his glasses from his nose. How he wished that he could retire. It was years since he had had a holiday.

A knock came upon the office door. Rat! Tat! 'Come in!'

Norman, the office vole, entered and stood there.

'Yes, Norman, what is it?'

'Please, Sir, it's Cap'n Bill Badger and Mister Izzybizzy to see you, Sir.'

Matty's round whiskered face lit up with pleasure.

'Show them in Norman, show them in at once!'

Cap'n Bill Badger and his shipmate Izzybizzy, the hedgehog, were very old friends of Matty's.

'Well! well! well!' exclaimed the vole as he extended his paw. 'What a nice surprise Cap'n Badger, and you too Izzy, it's a long time since we saw each other.'

Norman the office vole

Cap'n Bill Badger (or Uncle Bill as he was generally known) undid his tweed cloak and gave his deerstalker hat to Izzybizzy to hold. 'Nice to see you back at work, old friend,' said the badger heartily. 'Now, with the summer coming, you'll be a new vole.'

Matty sat back in his chair and shook his head, 'I don't feel it Cap'n Badger, but maybe I'll improve now that the sun shines. I expect you'll be wanting another boat? I heard your old one had been sunk.'

Uncle Bill nodded.

'Exactly, that's what I've come about. We feel we must be on the water again, there's nothing like boat life, you know, Matty.'

Matty smiled. 'Of course, I can quite understand that, Cap'n Badger. I suppose you were thinking of a new barge, eh? Well, we couldn't build you one in a hurry, you know, it would take all summer, it just couldn't be done.'

Uncle Bill nodded. 'We thought as much, Matty. No, our idea is (that's Izzy and me) that if we could raise our sunken barge the old *Wandering Wind* we might do something with her.'

Matty nodded. 'Well yes, Cap'n, you have something there. But I must warn you, the engine will be ruined, I can't install another, all that side of the business is done by a firm at Loudon Wharf, at a place called The World's End, on the Junction Canal.

'We could raise her in a morning with the necessary tackle, bring her back here to the boatyard, and when she's really dry, give her a fresh coat of paint.'

Uncle Bill thought for a moment. 'Worries me a bit, Matty, about not having an engine I mean, neither Izzy nor I like staying in one place.'

'Tell you what, Cap'n Badger,' said Matty, 'I could fit you up with an outboard. Of course, they're tricky things to start, but they'd push you along, I dare say. No doubt you could get her down to Loudon's at The World's End, and have a new inboard engine fitted there, how about that?'

'An excellent suggestion I do declare!' exclaimed Uncle Bill.

'Leave it to me then,' said the water vole laying a paw on the Badger's knee, 'I'll see my foreman this afternoon, he knows where your barge lies, and maybe this time next week we'll have it in the shed here, home and dry.'

Uncle Bill pumped Matty's paw in gratitude.

# CHAPTER TWO

Some days later our friends were up early to see how Matty was getting on.

Soon they saw before them the masts of the little boats in the yard.

Matty was out on the lawn talking to one of his work voles. Uncle Bill was shocked to see how thin and old his friend looked.

'Ah! Here you are Cap'n Badger, and Izzy,' Matty exclaimed. 'I have a little surprise for you!'

They followed him to the work sheds. There was the sound of hammering and singing and the smell of planed wood and fresh paint. Izzy, trotting behind Uncle Bill and Matty, was quivering

with excitement. 'There, what about her, Cap'n Badger?' Matty stood back with folded paws. Uncle Bill was speechless with admiration.

There, once more was their beloved barge, the *Wandering Wind*, gleaming, yes, fairly gleaming, with fresh paint!

Matty led the way into the saloon. Uncle Bill, as he looked around him, couldn't really believe it was their old *Wandering Wind*.

'Of course,' he said, 'We found the engine beyond hope, just scrap, Cap'n Badger, just scrap. But we've rigged you up with this new outboard engine. It'll push this old tub along all right, and we've put you in an extra bunk in case you want to take a passenger.'

'Ah, ha! Matty old friend,' Uncle Bill took Matty by the paw, 'that settles it then!'

'Settles what, Cap'n Badger?'

'We've decided that you must come with us to Loudon Wharf, Matty, it'll do you all the good in the world.'

Matty shook his head violently.

'No, no, Cap'n Badger, I'm behind

with my work as it is.'

A silence fell in the cabin. Outside the curtained windows a swallow darted by chattering happily.

Matty turned and faced Uncle Bill.

'Cap'n Badger, do you know *I think I'll come along with you after all*, I haven't had a holiday for years! Yes, old friend, dash it all, why shouldn't I!'

# CHAPTER THREE

What excitement when the day and hour came for their departure!

Every employee of Matty's turned out to wave goodbye. Norman, the office vole, ran up a Union Jack on the white mast on the quay.

Potter potter, glug glug, went the engine, the propellor making a boil of white under the stern.

Matty took the tiller and, with a nod and a wave to his work people, he slipped the *Wandering Wind* into gear and they moved slowly off. What a jolly send-off it all was!

Uncle Bill felt happier than he had done for many a day. He puffed at his pipe, scanning the familiar water meadows which were smoothly gliding by, and reflecting what an exciting thing life was!

'You take over, Cap'n Badger,' called Matty, 'Get the feel of her with this outboard, she yaws a bit, but you'll soon get the hang of it.'

Uncle Bill took hold of the tiller. The engine certainly *did* make a noise!

# CHAPTER FOUR

The next few days of travelling were peaceful enough.

They stopped when they felt like it for meals, or a spot of fishing, or just for a quiet snooze under pollarded willows.

Uncle Bill remarked to Izzy that Matty was looking a new vole already, fatter in the face, sleeker in coat, and brighter of eye, altogether a different animal!

On the evening of the fourth day they saw before them on the horizon a large town. 'That must be Brockle-hampton ahead,' said Matty, 'and I don't like large towns.'

Uncle Bill, who was steering, nodded,

'Couldn't agree more, Matty.'

'All the same,' piped up Izzy, 'I expect there are some good shops.'

Uncle Bill snorted, *'Shops!* Fine money wasters! I know what you are, Izzy, when you get near shops, you can't keep a penny in your pocket!'

What Uncle Bill said was true, Izzybizzy was a wasteful spender.

Before long the pleasant riverside meadows gave way to grimy warehouses. They passed under bridges where horrid little boys shouted rude things at them and laughed at Uncle Bill's deerstalker, and at Izzybizzy's hobby-nobby boots.

Both Uncle Bill and Matty had hoped to leave this town, with its grimy surroundings and ill-mannered inhabitants, far behind before nightfall. Alas!

It was not to be! They were barely through the main part of the town when some dirty coal barges, towed by one with a powerful engine, suddenly appeared round a bend of the canal.

Now, unfortunately, Matty had just handed the tiller over to Uncle Bill and had gone below decks. The barges came charging past and the little *Wandering Wind* tossed wildly in the wash.

It tossed so violently Uncle Bill could not control the rudder and the most terrible thing happened, *the outboard engine was shaken loose!*

There was a bang, a wild shout from Uncle Bill and the *Wandering Wind* drifted helplessly, engineless, and rudderless across the middle of the canal!

Matty's startled face appeared at

the cabin door. 'Gracious me, Cap'n Badger, we're in a mess now, never did like those outboards, always working loose, I should have secured it by a chain!'

The three animals felt quite helpless as the *Wandering Wind*, still with way on her, revolved gravely round and round in the middle of the canal. But, rescue was at hand. A friendly bargee rat threw them a rope, and managed to tow them into the bank where they tied up to a warehouse jetty.

There was nothing for it then but to make the best of a bad job, have supper, and discuss their plan of action.

Already lights were beginning to shine in the windows of the town, which made wavy reflections in the oily water.

After supper Uncle Bill and Matty went ashore to stretch their legs and Izzy was told to wash up the dirty dishes, much to his disgust, and his small heart rebelled.

Why shouldn't he go ashore too? He looked out of the cabin door. There was no sign of Uncle Bill and Matty. The violet dusk made a magic mystery of the gaily lit town.

Quickly Izzy went to his little cupboard in the corner and unhooked his best coat. Ramming his bobble-cap on his head and putting his bulging purse in his pocket, he scrambled ashore and set off along the wooden staging.

Between two dark warehouses there was a narrow alley-way. Beyond it he could see a brilliantly lit street with cars passing and re-passing and crowds

of people scurrying like ants. Izzy
needed no further invitation. His little
hobby-nobby boots rang out on the
tarred boarding of the quay, click!
clack! click! clack! He felt ready for
anything!

# CHAPTER FIVE

A busy town at night was a dangerous place for our Izzybizzy. You may also be wondering how he managed to look in at the shop windows. I will tell you!

He kept a look-out for any kindly lady he saw looking in at a shop window. Raising his bobble-cap he would ask very politely, if she would lift him up to see in.

And so it happened on this eventful evening. At every gaily lit window Izzy would wait until some lady chanced along and stopped to look. And always these kind and charming creatures would, if asked, accompany Izzy inside the shop and help him with his purchases whatever they might be!

Along the gaily lit street then, Izzy hurried, clutching his little leather purse tightly in one paw.

But, oh dear me! Izzy's sense of direction had never been strong. Very soon he realized he hadn't the slightest notion where the canal was! He was lost!

Suddenly padding footsteps sounded behind him. Izzy rolled up in a ball in the gutter petrified with terror. Some huge creature was blowing at his neck.

'Unroll, little hedgehog,' a gruff voice said kindly in his ear, 'You needn't be frightened of me, not of old Tatterdemalion, bless yer 'eart.'

Izzy unrolled just a little way and fixed a beady eye on the creature. This is what he saw, *a great shaggy sheep-dog!* Its ribs were showing, and it looked half-starved.

Izzy knew at once that this was a friendly dog, but a very poor one, a castaway dog, whom nobody loved.

'You shouldn't go about alone at night in Brocklehampton, sonny, not a little 'un like you. Where do you live?'

'I'm from the canal, on a barge called the *Wandering Wind*.' At last here was a friend.

Tatterdemalion sat down and put his big head on one side and spread out

his huge paws as props. 'Ah! Canal folk eh? Well now, the sooner you get back to the barge the better. If you come along with me I'll take you down to the canal, so you keep close to me.'

The two set off.

As they trotted along the lighted street Izzy had a job to keep up with his new friend. He was terrified of losing his way.

Suddenly Tatterdemalion stopped and lifted his shaggy nose, and Izzy noticed his ribs showing under the street lamp.

'Gosh, that's 'ard that is, mate!'

'What's hard, Tatters?'

'Can't you smell them pork chops?'

Izzy realized they had stopped outside a butcher's shop. His mind worked
quickly.

'Wait here, Tatters!'

He went boldly into the shop. A
comfortable looking woman was being
served with a pound of sausages. Izzy
tugged timidly at her skirt.

'Whatever do you want, my little
man?'

Izzy raised his bobble-cap.

'Please Ma'm, I want a pound of
sausages, here's the money.' He passed
up his purse. The butcher smiled, the
woman smiled.

'What a polite little thing!' she said

to the butcher, as Izzy trotted trium-
phantly out of the shop.

Tatterdemalion was sitting on the
edge of the pavement. His tongue was
hanging out. Izzy said nothing. He put
the sausages straight into Tatters'
mouth. There was a gulp, and they
were gone. Then Tatters sat back on

his haunches with a dreamy look in his eyes. Izzy felt a glow of pleasure.

'Come on, Izzy,' said Tatters at last, 'that was real good of you! I'll see you home, not far to go now. My! but I feel better for that!'

He gave a big shake, which started at his nose and finished at his tail, nearly lifting his hind legs off the ground.

'Yes,' thought Izzybizzy, 'very soon I'll be tucked up warm in my little bunk (after a good row with Cap'n Badger I expect), and poor Tatters here, where will *he* sleep?'

Izzy was just about to put this question when something quite extra-ordinary happened.

There was a screech of brakes. A big black van drew up beside them with two men in it.

'This is the one, Bill, this is 'im.'

Izzy had a fleeting glimpse of a large hand shooting out and grabbing Tatters by the scruff of his neck and bundling him into the van. The door slammed. The man came round to the driver's seat.

'Where are you taking him?' squeaked Izzy, beside himself with grief and anxiety.

'Dog's home, little 'un, can't have stray dogs loose in this town. Don't you carry on neither, or we'll take you along too,' said the man as Izzy started to cry.

The van started up. Izzy saw its red tail-light vanish down the street. He clung to the nearest lamp post, sobbing his heart out.

He didn't know which way to go, all he wanted was to find Tatters and somehow get help to him.

Soon, quite tired out, he came to a little town square and found a seat under some spreading chestnut trees. A street lamp cast shadows from its newly opened leaves which made weaving patterns on the path.

'What shall I do? what shall I do?' moaned Izzy, 'I can't go back to the barge, I *must* find Tatters!'

One after another the lights were going out in the houses, shutting like eyes, as curtains were drawn and people went to bed. A church clock struck eleven. Goodness! How the time had flown by! But Izzy was too miserable to care.

As he sat there, he thought he heard

music far away, a squeaky kind of music as though someone was playing a concertina. Someone was singing too. Izzy was alert at once. There was something familiar in that distant sound of music, surely it couldn't be, *it couldn't be?*

He strained his eyes. A figure was coming down the path under the chestnut trees, a small ragged figure. It was a rat. Around his neck was a notice 'Pity the Blind'. On his head was a cap many sizes too large for him. His pointed whiskered nose was raised in the air and he was singing at the top of his voice and at the same time playing the concertina, or squeeze-box, slung in front of him.

Izzy found himself trembling, not with fear, oh, dear no, but with joy.

This stranger, could be none other than their old pal, Beggar Rat, who had a knack of appearing whenever they were in trouble.

Beggar Rat was a friend of all 'down-and-outs' and from the rich of the world he wheedled and whined many an odd penny. And, I might add, despite the notice round his neck, he could see perfectly well!

Izzy found himself smiling for the first time that night as he watched his friend's approach. He, if anyone, would be able to help to trace Tatterdemalion. So Izzy curled up in the corner of the seat, under the quietly moving shadows of the chestnut leaves, and sat waiting.

Beggar Rat drew nearer, his long whiskered nose uplifted in the spring night. And this is the song he sang:

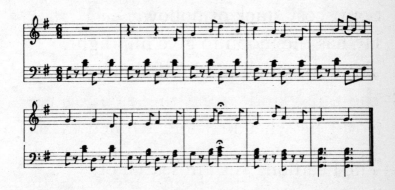

A beggar leads a jolly life
He has no need of money
He doesn't even want a wife,
Just something in his tummy!

He hears the early song of bird,
He smells the sweet wind blowing,
He need not heed a master's word,
Or work when it is snowing.

His house may be (just for the
    night)
Some cosy stack or hollow,
He has the moon to give him light,
To show which road to follow.


The headlong rush in search of
    gold,
The torment of the 'rush hour',
Give him the blue hills, fold on fold,
The evening peace, the 'hush' hour.


The autumn lane, the misty wood,
The berries on the thorn,
The cloven print where deer have
    stood,
To watch the flush of dawn.

And so kind friends, please shed no
    tear
For Beggar Rat in tatters,
He's his own master, never fear,
It's how you live that matters!

Though the rat's eyes were very sharp he did not appear to notice Izzy. He came and sat on the opposite end of the seat and sang the song to its close. Then Beggar Rat unslung his squeeze box putting it down beside him.

'Beggar Rat!' exclaimed Izzy, 'You don't know how glad I am to see you!'

The rat pretended to be startled. 'Why goodness me, if it isn't Izzybizzy ... Izzybizzy all by himself in the middle of Brocklehampton!'

Then Izzy told Beggar Rat all about the *Wandering Wind* and Matty and how the engine had broken down just on the outskirts of the town. He told him how he had got fed up with being ordered about and made to wash up the supper things whilst Matty and Uncle Bill went off for a walk.

The rat heard him through from beginning to end.

'Well Izzy, I can't say I blame you, little people often get pushed around by bigger ones, it'll teach 'em a lesson not to take things for granted.

'Now, about this new friend of yours, Tatters whats-'is-name? As you know, I avoid dogs whenever I can, but from what you say about poor old Tatters, he's a homeless wanderer, just like myself.'

'Why should they want to take him away, Beggar Rat?'

'Oh, stray dogs in towns are a nuisance, I shouldn't give much for his chances, not if they took him off in a black van.'

Izzy got up from the seat and took Beggar Rat by his ragged sleeve.

'Look, Beggar Rat, we must do something, *PLEASE!*'

The rat sat thoughtfully for a moment playing with his tail, the tip of which was missing (it had been chopped off years before in a scuffle with some pirate cats).

Over the sleeping city a clock tolled twelve strokes. To Izzy they seemed to be tolling for his poor old friend Tatters.

'Very well, Izzy, we'll see what can be done, I've a pretty shrewd idea where he might be. You just bide quiet for a bit.'

# CHAPTER SIX

Izzy found it terribly hard to sit there on the seat with Beggar Rat, never had time seemed to move so slowly!

But at last the rat got up from the seat, stretched, then, picking up the concertina, he slung it across his back.

'Now listen to me, Izzy,' he said in a low voice, 'you keep one step behind me, there are still a few people about and if I see a policeman we'll dodge down a side road, because I haven't a street trading licence and singing is against the law.'

The rat kept off the main lighted highways, he seemed to know the town backwards. After what seemed ages and *miles* of hard pavements they came to a high wall overhung with plane trees.

At the end of the road was a tall dark building. Beggar Rat stopped and held up a paw. Izzy heard a sound which made his prickles rise, a low moaning noise. He clutched Beggar Rat's sleeve.

'Whatever's that?'

'It's the lost dogs in the dogs' home,' whispered Beggar Rat.

'Are there more than one then?' gasped Izzy.

'Sure, all the strays are brought here.'

'Will Tatters be there too, in the dogs' prison?'

The rat nodded. 'Sure he'll be there, poor devil.'

'What are we going to do?' whispered Izzy.

'Go in of course! But, if you don't mind, I'll keep out of sight, if they saw me they'd forget all about being locked up and raise merry hell.'

Very cautiously Beggar Rat squeezed under a green gate. Izzy followed. In front of them was a winding drive-way fringed with gloomy laurels. The house was in complete darkness. It had ivy on the walls and a large notice, which said 'Dogs' Home' over the door.

The rat, followed by Izzybizzy, crept along in the shadow of the laurel hedge, until they came to an entrance to a yard. Inside Izzy could see iron palings and a row of pens, each with a kennel.

Beggar Rat's long whiskered nose came close to Izzy's ear. 'Right. Now listen, Izzy. You creep along in the shadow of the wall there until you find Tatters' pen. Explain to him that I'm a friend of yours, and that we'll find some way of getting him out.'

Izzy gulped, and nodded, then set off along the bottom of the wall, just as Beggar Rat had told him.

# CHAPTER SEVEN

With beating heart Izzy crept along in the shadow.

Soon he saw, in the nearest pen, an enormous creature, a cross, maybe, between a labrador and a sheep dog. It was bigger than Tatterdemalion. This was the one which had been making all the noise. His ears were cocked, and now and again he lifted his muzzle skywards and howled most fearfully, showing the whites of his eyes. There was another little dog, a terrier, beside him, sitting in a hopeless sort of huddle by the bars.

They never saw Izzy creeping along. Izzy could hear what the little one was saying to his companion.

'You won't do any good making all that racket, Big Job. The man will get up and beat us.'

'He'll do more than that to us in the morning, Banjo. We'll be taken away and finished off, and that goes for all of us.'

'Making a noise won't help,' replied Banjo. 'He'll finish us off all the sooner!'

Six months before Banjo had worked in a circus, and knew all kinds of amusing tricks, but he had run away with a lady friend.

Big Job, for that was the big dog's name, lifted up his nose and howled again.

'Look at Tatterdemalion,' went on the little dog reprovingly, '*He* hasn't said a word since he came in, he's pretending to be asleep. Fat Fred's with him, they're lying together but *they* don't make a noise.'

Big Job turned his head and looked into the next run.

Tatterdemalion was stretched out on his side, his ribs clearly visible in the starlight. By him was a long-bodied dog, a Basset hound. It had brown floppy ears and a wrinkled forehead. It was licking Tatterdemalion's nose.

Izzy crept along the wall until he was opposite their pen.

Fat Fred, the basset hound, unlike the others, wasn't at all thin. The fact is, like Tatterdemalion, he had been sold by his owners to somebody else in a distant part of the country and had escaped to find his way home and had been picked up by the police. Nobody had claimed him, and like most of the other poor lost dogs, no one had wanted to buy him.

Tatterdemalion's brown eyes were wide open. He rather liked the feel of Fat Fred's warm tongue. Fat Fred could smell sausages, that's why he was licking Tatterdemalion's muzzle.

All at once Fat Fred stopped licking.

'Funny thing, Tatters, I smell something I can't put a name to, it isn't rabbit, it isn't rat, it's rather a nice meaty smell, and it certainly isn't sausage, it has something of hedge bottoms about it.'

Tatterdemalion's ear lifted, his experienced nose began to twitch too.

'I tell you what that smell is, Fat Fred, its hedgehog, that's what it is.

I met a lost hedgehog in the town to-night. Lost he was.'

Fat Fred and Tatters poked their noses between the iron bars. 'I can see the top of his head,' said Tatters, 'I'd know that bobble-cap anywhere!'

Izzybizzy stood up on the tips of his hobby-nobby boots.

'Don't make a noise, Tatters,' he whispered, overjoyed to see his old pal again. 'My friend Beggar Rat's here, no need to worry. I've never known Beggar Rat be beaten by anything!'

Now all this time the rat had been watching from the shadow of the laurels and when he saw the hedgehog deep in conversation with Tatters he slipped up behind and tugged at Izzy's coat.

'Tell 'em to keep quiet,' hissed the rat.

'This is Beggar Rat, I told you about,' said Izzy, 'he's as clever as clever!'

By this time Big Job and Banjo were also standing up on their hind legs against the bars listening to the conversation, and a third dog, an ancient spaniel called Benbow, had emerged from his kennel and was listening too. (Benbow was blind in one eye after a fight with a cat.)

Beggar Rat unslung his concertina and put it carefully down beside him.

Everybody sat quite still watching him. Ten ears were cocked expectantly, you could have heard a bat squeak. Beggar Rat stood back and surveyed the iron door of Tatters' run. It looked like this.

Near the top was a simple drop catch

on the outside.

'Tell Tatters to stand on his hind legs,' whispered the rat, 'and push his nose as far as it will go between the bars.'

Tatters did as he was told. His nose projected about two inches. Beggar Rat stood back judging the distance. Then he took a little backward step. To the astonishment of everyone the next moment he was standing on tip-toe on Tatters' nose. He reached up with his pink claws and pushed up the catch. The door swung open! Tatters and Fat Fred were free!

'Hey! What about us, mate?' Came an urgent hoarse whisper from Big Job, 'you can't leave us behind!'

'Shut up both of you,' Tatters gave a grin, his lips curled back, he was really smiling.

'You don't think we'd go off and leave you do you, you chumps!' He stood up against the gate of their pen and nodded to Beggar Rat who shinned up his tail, clambered to the top of his head and released the catch in the same way. Out rushed Big Job and Benbow, beside themselves with delight.

Izzy had no time to put on his boots. He frantically snatched them up and ran. Everybody tore down the winding drive Big Job was first, then Benbow and Fat Fred, followed by Banjo, Tatter-demalion, and Beggar Rat. Bringing up the rear, was poor Izzy. Tatter-demalion turned back at once.

'Quick, climb up on my back, hold on tightly.' He took Izzy's hobby-nobby boots in his mouth, and the hedgehog gripped the shaggy fur

around his neck with teeth and claws.
Away they went at a rattling pace,

Izzy swaying and gasping, riding old
Tatters like a diminutive jockey.

# CHAPTER EIGHT

We must leave Izzybizzy and the others for the moment and see what happened back at the canal after Izzy had left the barge.

When Uncle Bill and Matty set off for their walk at a brisk pace they soon left the town behind them. They followed the towpath beside the canal.

'How can we ever reach Loudon Wharf without an engine?' asked Uncle Bill, as they walked along, 'It's still some way from here, we cannot row the barge, maybe we could get a tow?' Matty shook his head. 'No barges go beyond this town. That's why they call Loudon Wharf "The World's

End" . . . it's the end of the canal arm.'

'The only course open to us is to beg a tow back to my place at Compton Verney. It will mean a delay of a week or so.'

'Well,' said the badger, 'let us sleep on it, Matty, it's getting late, and Izzy will be wondering where we are.'

They hurried back along the towpath. As they drew near the moored barge Uncle Bill was puzzled to see no sign of life.

'Izzy must have turned in, Matty, we will have a noggin of hot cocoa before we go to bed, I think, the walk has made me thirsty.'

Uncle Bill climbed aboard and Matty followed. He pushed open the cabin door. It was so dark he had to strike a match. By its fading fluttering light he was astonished to find both the cabin and Izzy's bunk empty. Greatly mystified, he lit the lantern which hung from the cabin ceiling.

'He's washed up the supper things anyway,' said Uncle Bill, poking his nose into the galley, 'I do believe he's gone off into the town on one of his spending sprees. I find this extremely annoying of him, disobedient too!'

Matty kept silent. This was no business of his.

Uncle Bill brewed up some cocoa and he and Matty sat drinking it in the saloon under the hanging lantern. The hours passed, still no Izzybizzy! Uncle Bill looked anxious.

'I don't like it, Matty, he should have been in long ago, why, the shops shut at six o'clock!' The badger got up uneasily.

They went up on deck and scanned the dock side, but it lay empty under the stars. He was about to step ashore when from the direction of the town came a drumming sound, as of many feet running. From between the warehouses emerged what appeared to be a pack of ravening wolves.

First came Big Job, pounding along, his ears flying, his tail streaming. Then came Banjo, Benbow, and Fat Fred, neck and neck, and finally, Tatter-demalion with a small object perched on his back waving his bobble-cap. Hanging on to the tip of his tail was Beggar Rat burdened with his squeeze-box, clinging on for dear life, and at times becoming airborne.

Uncle Bill, who had had many weird and surprising experiences during his long life, both on the canal (and off it) stood utterly dumbfounded. He never trusted dogs. But, tails were wagging, everyone who could grin, grinned.

Izzybizzy dismounted from his un-certain perch by sliding down Tatters' tail.

With a furtive eye on Cap'n Badger he sat down and began to lace up his boots with many grunts and puffs.

Beggar Rat now appeared, complete with concertina, from behind the pack of dogs.

'Ah!' exclaimed the badger with vast relief. 'Goodness me, it's Beggar

Rat, *now* we shall get some explanation!'

'For heaven's sake, Beggar Rat, I'm glad to see you! DO explain what all this is about and what all these dogs are doing here!

So, Beggar Rat told Uncle Bill all he knew.

Uncle Bill listened patiently to the rat's story, nodding his head from time to time and saying 'uh, hu', just so, and extraordinary! And, now and again looking at Izzybizzy who seemed to be taking a very long time to lace up his hobby-nobby boots.

'Well, my good Beggar Rat,' Uncle Bill said, when the rat had told him all, 'since you have got Izzy out of a terrible mess, what suggestion have you now? We have no engine and no chance of

getting one, and we are a long way from Loudon Wharf, even if we had one.'

The rat sat down and played with his tail for a moment or two, a good sign for it meant he was thinking.

Then he came aboard the *Wandering Wind* and drew Uncle Bill aside.

'Now, Cap'n Badger,' he said in a low voice, 'I've thought out a scheme. We can't abandon these poor starving dogs. If they stay in the town any longer it will be the end of all of them.'

The badger nodded, wondering what on earth was in the rat's mind.

'Well, my idea is this, Cap'n Badger. You have lost your engine, right? Well, I have a plan for getting to Loudon Wharf! You know of course that, in the old days, barges were drawn by horses, correct?'

Uncle Bill nodded.

'Well then, here we have two powerful big dogs, Tatterdemalion and Big Job, to say nothing of Benbow, Fat Fred, and Banjo. Let us harness them to the barge, and let them tow us!'

Uncle Bill gazed at the rat with wonder and gratitude. 'Beggar Rat!' he exclaimed, 'you *are* a wonder, this is a magnificent idea!'

'Good,' said the rat, much gratified, 'then let me talk to the dogs and put my suggestion to them.'

He gathered them around him in a circle whilst Uncle Bill and Matty stood expectantly waiting.

Then the rat returned to the barge with a wide grin on his cunning whiskered face.

'It's O.K., Cap'n Badger, they think it's a smashing idea, they want to start right away.'

Uncle Bill was overjoyed.

# CHAPTER NINE

As the stars of night began to fade a strange procession made its way along the canal. Tatterdemalion and Big Job in the lead, Banjo, Benbow, and Fat Fred, grasping the tow rope in their teeth, and the *Wandering Wind* herself forging ahead at a good pace with Uncle Bill at the tiller.

Izzybizzy, quite worn out and exhausted with the night's adventure had been sent to bed. Matty sat beside Uncle Bill enjoying the fresh air. Beggar Rat sat cross-pawed on the cabin roof, his cap on one side, playing his squeeze-box. Nobody could tire *him* out.

So all that day the *Wandering Wind* made good progress.

At last, towards evening, they saw before them a cluster of trees, an old grey church tower peeping above some huge chestnuts.

'We'll stop there and have a meal,' said Uncle Bill, 'so, heave ho my hearties!'

They moored the barge under a willow and the dogs flung themselves down on a daisy bank, quite exhausted, with their tongues hanging.

Uncle Bill went up into the village to find a butcher's shop.

Soon the Badger was seen returning. 'The butcher was more than generous, Matty,' he said, throwing down a sack

on the towpath, 'I told him I had a pack of starving homeless dogs who had done us a good turn. Couldn't do enough for us. Now we'll find some nice quiet lay-by off the main canal, and give everyone a really good supper, how about that?'

They found the ideal place a mile beyond the village, a peaceful spot called a 'pound' where, in the old days, the barges used to pass each other. It was covered with water-lilies and hedged in by tall reeds, which screened them from prying eyes. It was a perfect ending to a perfect day.

When all their tummies were full Beggar Rat sang the new song he had composed for just such an occasion. This is what he sang:

## This Is The Hour

This is the hour the nightjar spins,
When cries the hunting owl,
When linnets sleep deep in their
  whins
And Alley cats do prowl.

This is the hour when work is done,
Bird, beast, and humble kine,
All seek their beds, yes, everyone,
And I will go seek mine!

When Beggar Rat had finished he looked around him, expectantly, for applause. All his audience were asleep!

# CHAPTER TEN

Next day the gallant 'barge pack' made good progress, and towed the boat along at a steady pace.

They made frequent stops to rest the dogs, and soon the exercise made them as hungry as ever.

They reached the village of Weston-in-the-Hedges towards the end of the afternoon. There they moored in the shelter of a small spinney where birds sang loudly and cuckoos were calling. Some two hundred yards distant they could see a red-brick canal bridge which carried the road to the village.

Izzy was allowed ashore into a near-by meadow to gather cowslips for the cabin table, and solemnly promised he would not stray away.

Soon he heard, far off, the puffing and panting of some enormous steam engine.

If you have already met Izzy in other books you will know that he was passionately fond of all kinds of steam engines. Yet, there was no railway within miles of the village of Weston-in-the-Hedges! Izzy wondered if he was dreaming. Yet, as he listened, the panting and the chuffing grew louder, and in a moment or two he saw steam over the hedgerow elms higher up the road. It seemed that a convoy of sorts, was approaching the bridge.

'How very curious,' said Izzybizzy aloud (he had a habit of talking to himself), 'it must be a steam roller.'

Soon he made out a tall brass-bound

funnel, above the hedge tops, and a big flywheel, and a cylinder puffing clouds of steam.

'OOO!' Izzy let out a hoot of ecstasy. . . . 'How I wish it would stop, just for a minute or two, OOOO! There's more than one.' Soon he could see a second funnel!

Each steam traction engine was towing a string of vans, big vans, like small houses on wheels. By now Izzy was trembling with excitement. Imagine his feelings when, with a lot of shouting and a cloud of steam, the whole cavalcade came to a stop just short of the bridge where there was a wide grass margin.

Some men climbed down from the footplate and put a big pipe down into the canal.

'Ah!' said Izzy, 'they are taking on some water, I must see about this!'

Quite forgetting about the others, who would by now be getting supper ready, he hurried along the towpath to the bridge and so up to the road. He walked all round the engines gazing upwards. How the bright copper glowed in the evening light, just catching the last rays of the sinking sun!

What a beautiful green the boiler was, bound in its shining bands, that massive flywheel, the spittings and hissings from the boiler!!

It was not until he had thoroughly examined this splendid monster that he happened to glance at the big train of vans. On the sides were pictures of lions and tigers all painted in gay colours and decorative lettering which said

'BARNABY BARNUM'S CIRCUS', in bright scarlet letters!

Izzy hurried along to the next engine which was waiting down the road. The driver was not too busy and had time to talk.

'Hullo, youngster, coming to the circus?'

'Where?' cried Izzy eagerly.

'Brocklehampton of course, sonny, never 'eard of Brocklehampton Feast Week?'

Izzy's heart sank. Brocklehampton! He'd forgotten all about it! That hateful place! He shook his head.

'No, Mister, I can't go to no circus, we're on the canal, see, and we're on our way to Loudon Wharf for a new engine to be fitted.'

'Ah,' said the man lolling on the

wheel, 'pity, that's a real shame that is, you'd like our circus, travel all over the country we do, giving shows . . . seen the elephants?'

'What elephants?'

'Why *our* elephants of course, Susie and Shiner, they're at the end of the vans.'

Izzy ran along to the end of the procession. There to be sure were two elephants as big as cottages!

How huge they were, what enormous feet, what little intelligent eyes!

One of them put its trunk down to Izzy. Before he knew what was happening he found himself sailing up through the air, hobby-nobby boots and all, and deposited on top of the elephant's head. It placed him there as gently as a lady places a precious piece of china on a shelf.

Izzy spluttered and gasped. He was *miles* from the ground. Somebody on the road below began laughing. He was a jolly red-faced man, who took the part of a clown in the circus. He had a scarlet kerchief round his neck. ''Ere Sarah, come and see what our Susie's got on top of 'er 'ead!'

A handsome young woman came out of one of the vans and stood with her hands on her hips. She took one look at Izzy on Susie's head and started to giggle, then she began to laugh and laugh, 'hee! hee! hee!' bending double. 'Ho! Ho! Ho!' laughed the jolly man. They laughed until the tears were running down their cheeks. And it certainly *was* a comical sight, poor little Izzy in his bobble-cap and his hobby-nobby boots, placed up there on the elephant's head crying to get down.

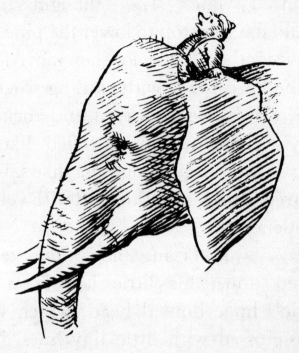

The van in front gave a jolt, from the bridge there was a sound of puffing, and to Izzy's dismay the elephant began to move. 'Let me down! let me down!' he squealed, hanging on to the elephant's ear.

Unfortunately only the first engine required water. Izzy thought they would have to stop to lower the pipe for the second one, but no, they moved on to the hard road, with rattling wheels. The van in front swayed and rocked. Izzy's elephant, Susie, rolled like a ship at sea, but her huge feet, like sawn-off tree trunks, trod the road with velvet gentleness.

Izzy was crying now, the tears rolled down his little jacket on to Susie's huge domed head, which was criss-crossed with little tiny lines, like cracks in baked clay, and it had wisps of coarse hair to which Izzy was obliged to cling or he would certainly have fallen off.

Bridge and canal were left behind, so was the village of Weston-in-the-

Hedges.

Barnaby Barnum's Circus was on the move. Izzy was going with it.

# CHAPTER ELEVEN

Uncle Bill began to get worried when Izzy did not return.

'Matty, you had better go and see if young Izzy has fallen in, or gone to sleep. He's very quiet, I should have thought he would have looked in to see how we were getting on. What was that puffing noise I heard in the distance? I didn't know there was a railway near.'

'I've been listening to it for some time,' said Banjo, whose ears had been cocked for some minutes past. 'I think they must be ploughing somewhere with the old steam ploughs. Funny I can't hear it now.'

Everyone listened but the wind was wrong, it was blowing towards the bridge.

Uncle Bill shook Matty by the shoulder, 'Matty, be a good vole, and just go and see if you can find young Izzy.'

Matty soon came bustling back through the bushes in a terrible state.

'Cap'n Badger! Izzy's gone! There's no trace of him!' The badger gave a groan, 'Oh *no*! Matty, don't say he's gone off again!'

Everyone crowded on to the tow-path. Beggar Rat went one way with Big Job, Tatters, and Benbow, Uncle Bill, Fat Fred, and Banjo went as far as the bridge. Banjo squeezed under the fence and sniffed about.

'Come here, Cap'n Badger, there are

lots of big tyre marks on the grass and there's something else,' Banjo stopped and sniffed the air, 'I'd know that smell anywhere!'

'I can smell something too,' said Uncle Bill, who had a good nose himself, 'but I can't put a name to it.'

Banjo sat down, his eyes were full of tears, his nose kept jerking up, snuff, snuff, snuff. 'Oh dear,' said Banjo, 'silly of me, but do you know, Cap'n Badger, it was a smell I came to know so well during my circus days, it's elephants!! It's elephants right enough, no other creature leaves a spoor like that.'

'Elephants or not Banjo, where's Izzy, we *must* find him . . .'

Uncle Bill never finished his sentence. Banjo, who had been standing gazing into the sunset, sniffing and sniffing, set off down the road as hard as he could go.

The old loved smells of the travelling circus were flooding across the fields to him.

'Banjo!' called Uncle Bill cupping his paws. 'BANJO!' But Banjo took no heed. Smaller and smaller became that little fleeing figure until a bend in the road hid him from view.

'We won't see *him* again,' said Fat Fred with conviction peering into the gathering shadows, 'he's circus mad that dog is!'

# CHAPTER TWELVE

Tatterdemalion, who all this time had been sitting on the towpath listening to the badger, gave himself one of his big shakes.

'I'll go find him, Cap'n Badger, that circus outfit wouldn't go much farther tonight. You bring the barge on to Loudon Wharf, I'll find Izzy, and come after you.'

Uncle Bill shook his head. 'Don't bother, Tatters, he isn't worth it,' he added bitterly. The badger checked himself and was silent. He knew in his heart he loved his little shipmate.

'Oh, *very well,* Tatters, come on you others, we'll get moving.'

The dogs gripped the rope in their teeth.

Slowly, they moved away under the bridge, and out into the country beyond.

And so that anxious night wore away to dawn as the barge moved onwards.

At last the towpath took a turn to the right, some buildings loomed up ahead, and a grove of Lombardy poplars marked their journey's end.

'That's it!' cried Matty, 'that's Loudon Wharf at the World's End!'

'There's something on the towpath, Matty!' called Uncle Bill who was looking through his binoculars, 'I believe it's . . . it's Tatters, yes, and there's someone with him, yes Matty, it's Izzybizzy!'

'Well done, Tatters!' exclaimed

Uncle Bill, he's found him! I thought he would!'

Slowly the barge came to a stop. Izzybizzy was leaning against the big dog's front leg, looking very ashamed of himself, and *very* tired. Tatters was grinning widely.

'Thought I'd find him, Cap'n Badger, found him in the van with the lion tamer who wanted Izzy to join 'em in the elephant act or something. But you won't see Banjo again, it's his old outfit, Barnaby Barnum's Circus, the one he used to work with.'

Uncle Bill said nothing for a moment or two.

'Well, Izzy,' he said gruffly, 'you'd better come aboard and tuck up in your bunk, it's all ready for you!'

There's really little more to tell about this eventful voyage to The World's End by our two old friends, Uncle Bill and Izzybizzy.

The inboard engine was duly installed, and the return journey passed without incident. Big Job went south to find his master, and Banjo is, I hear, one of the star turns in Barnaby Barnum's Circus.

Sometimes Uncle Bill and Izzybizzy, on their journeyings up and down the canal call in at Matty's place to chat about old times.

The three dogs, Tatters, Fat Fred, and poor old half-blind Benbow, have settled down well. Matty says that Tatters makes a splendid guard dog. Apart from helping with the boats they have good food and a fire to sit by in winter. Their coats shine like the morning sun. Tatters' ribs are quite invisible, you would never believe he is the same gaunt spectre which once roamed the back streets of Brockle-hampton. Fat Fred is fatter than ever, if that were possible.

The only grumble Matty has (and that's a very little one) is that he has to pay for three dog licences each year. He says it's worth it.

## *THE END*

*'BB'*

## *THE LITTLE GREY MEN*

Dodder, Baldmoney, Cloudberry and Sneeze-wort, are the last gnomes left in Britain and they live by a Warwickshire brook. Their home is under an oak tree which grows on the banks of the Folly.

When Cloudberry, the restless one, sets out to explore the Folly to its source, he doesn't return. The story of *The Little Grey Men* begins when his three brothers build a boat and set out to find him.

*The Little Grey Men* won the Carnegie Medal and is beautifully illustrated by the author.

'BB'

# THE LITTLE GREY MEN GO DOWN THE BRIGHT STREAM

The last gnomes in England, Dodder, Bald-money, Cloudberry and Sneezewort are peace-fully sleeping winter away in the old oak tree when they hear a frantic knocking at the door. Someone is desperate to wake them for Folly brook is drying up. They will have to do some-thing, and quickly . . .

The sequel to *The Little Grey Men*, winner of the Carnegie Medal.

*Sid Fleischman*

## *THE MIDNIGHT HORSE*

When Touch arrives in Cricklewood (population 217 – 216 Fine Folks and one Infernal Grouch) it's just Touch's bad luck that the Infernal Grouch is his only surviving relative, wicked great-uncle Judge Wigglesforth.

The judge gives Touch a cold and cheating welcome and Touch prefers to run away rather than wait for great-uncle to put him in the orphanage. He knows one person who can help him, The Great Chaffalo, who can create horses with a bit of straw and a touch of midnight . . .

'What Leon Garfield does for Victorian England, medallist Fleischman, does for the Red Raven Inn . . . a deftly told story of innocence and villainy.' *Publishers' Weekly*

By the author of *The Whipping Boy*, winner of the 1987 Newbery Medal.

*Kenneth Grahame*

## THE WIND IN THE WILLOWS

*Everything was very still now. The dusk advanced on him steadily, rapidly, gathering in behind and before; and the light seemed to be draining away like flood-water. Then the faces began . . .*

The Wild Wood seems a terrifying place to Mole, lost and alone. But it is also full of friends – kind lazy Badger who shelters him from the snow-storm, brave and lively Ratty and the irrespon-sible Mr Toad, famous for his fortune and car smashes. And when Toad Hall is captured by hostile weasels and stoats, the friends know they must fight together to survive . . .

*Dodie Smith*

# THE HUNDRED AND ONE DALMATIANS

'Wouldn't they make enchanting fur coats?' said Cruella to her husband.

When their fifteen puppies suddenly disappear, Pongo and Missis know the hideous Cruella de Vil is responsible. The fearless Pongo and brave Missis set out to recover their family. Dogs across the country help them in their dangerous adventure but soon they discover that there are rather more than just fifteen dalmatians whose lives are threatened by Cruella.

# A selected list of titles available from Mammoth

While every effort is made to keep prices low, it is sometimes necessary to increase prices at short notice. Mandarin Paperbacks reserves the right to show new retail prices on covers which may differ from those previously advertised in the text or elsewhere.

The prices shown below were correct at the time of going to press.

| | | | | |
|---|---|---|---|---|
| ☐ | 7497 0366 0 | **Dilly the Dinosaur** | Tony Bradman | £2.50 |
| ☐ | 7497 0137 4 | **Flat Stanley** | Jeff Brown | £2.50 |
| ☐ | 7497 0306 7 | **The Chocolate Touch** | P Skene Catling | £2.50 |
| ☐ | 7497 0568 X | **Dorrie and the Goblin** | Patricia Coombs | £2.50 |
| ☐ | 7497 0114 5 | **Dear Grumble** | W J Corbett | £2.50 |
| ☐ | 7497 0054 8 | **My Naughty Little Sister** | Dorothy Edwards | £2.50 |
| ☐ | 7497 0723 2 | **The Little Prince (colour ed.)** | A Saint-Exupery | £3.99 |
| ☐ | 7497 0305 9 | **Bill's New Frock** | Anne Fine | £2.99 |
| ☐ | 7497 0590 6 | **Wild Robert** | Diana Wynne Jones | £2.50 |
| ☐ | 7497 0661 9 | **The Six Bullerby Children** | Astrid Lindgren | £2.50 |
| ☐ | 7497 0319 9 | **Dr Monsoon Taggert's Amazing Finishing Academy** | Andrew Matthews | £2.50 |
| ☐ | 7497 0420 9 | **I Don't Want To!** | Bel Mooney | £2.50 |
| ☐ | 7497 0833 6 | **Melanie and the Night Animal** | Gillian Rubinstein | £2.50 |
| ☐ | 7497 0264 8 | **Akimbo and the Elephants** | A McCall Smith | £2.50 |
| ☐ | 7497 0048 3 | **Friends and Brothers** | Dick King-Smith | £2.50 |
| ☐ | 7497 0795 X | **Owl Who Was Afraid of the Dark** | Jill Tomlinson | £2.99 |

All these books are available at your bookshop or newsagent, or can be ordered direct from the publisher. Just tick the titles you want and fill in the form below.

**Mandarin Paperbacks**, Cash Sales Department, PO Box 11, Falmouth, Cornwall TR10 9EN.

Please send cheque or postal order, no currency, for purchase price quoted and allow the following for postage and packing:

UK including BFPO    £1.00 for the first book, 50p for the second and 30p for each additional book ordered to a maximum charge of £3.00.

Overseas including Eire    £2 for the first book, £1.00 for the second and 50p for each additional book thereafter.

NAME (Block letters) ................................................................................................................

ADDRESS ................................................................................................................................

................................................................................................................................................

☐ I enclose my remittance for ........................

☐ I wish to pay by Access/Visa Card Number

Expiry Date